MW01178966

WHITEWATER RAFTING

BY SARA GREEN

BELLWETHER MEDIA · MINNEAPOLIS, MN

Jump into the cockpit and take flight with Pilot books. Your journey will take you on high-energy adventures as you learn about all that is wild, weird, fascinating, and fun!

This edition first published in 2014 by Bellwether Media, Inc.

No part of this publication may be reproduced in whole or in part without written permission of the publisher. For information regarding permission, write to Bellwether Media, Inc., Attention: Permissions Department, 5357 Penn Avenue South, Minneapolis, MN 55419.

Library of Congress Cataloging-in-Publication Data

Green, Sara, 1964-
  Whitewater Rafting / by Sara Green.
    pages cm. – (Pilot: Outdoor Adventures)
  Includes bibliographical references and index.
  Summary: "Engaging images accompany information about whitewater rafting. The combination of high-interest subject matter and narrative text is intended for students in grades 3 through 7"– Provided by publisher.
  ISBN 978-1-62617-087-2 (hardcover : alk. paper)
  1. Rafting (Sports) I. Title.
  GV780.G74 2014
  797.12'1–dc23
                    2013038524

Printed in the United States of America, North Mankato, MN.

TABLE OF CONTENTS

RUNNING THE RAPIDS

A whitewater raft lightly bounces over riffles in a river. Six passengers sit on the sides of the raft. Each person holds a paddle. At the back is the guide. He is an experienced rafter and knows how to steer the boat safely. As the raft drifts, the passengers marvel at the stunning canyon walls that rise around them.

The riffles get stronger and the current begins to move swiftly. Ahead, the passengers see rapids. The water flows so quickly that it looks white. The raft enters the rapids, and waves splash onto the passengers. Their hearts race. "Forward!" shouts the guide. The passengers dig their paddles into the water and pull hard. The guide steers the raft around rocks. He directs it through a safe passage. Soon, the raft enters calm water again. The passengers can hardly wait to see what is around the next bend. They are excited to run more rapids!

Whitewater is a powerful, turbulent flow of water. It is found in rapids, waterfalls, and other fast-moving parts of rivers. In whitewater rafting, people paddle through flowing water in inflatable boats called rafts. They use paddles and oars to steer the rafts down the river and through rapids.

Thousands of people go whitewater rafting each year. Many enjoy the thrill of running the rapids. Others prefer a calm ride down a lazy river. They watch the scenery and look for wildlife. People of all ages can go whitewater rafting. Many enjoy spending the day or just a few hours on a river. Others choose multi-day trips. These rafters paddle during the day and camp along the river at night. Many hike and explore the area when they are not on the water.

Reading the River

Rafters must be able to recognize the direction of the current and see any dangers. This skill, called reading the river, allows them to plan a safe route.

WHITEWATER RAFTS

Whitewater rafts come in different shapes and sizes. A typical raft has room for four to ten rafters and an experienced guide. The guide steers the raft and gives instructions. Rafts come with footholds and handholds to help people stay on board. Many rafters use **dry bags** to keep personal belongings from getting wet. These and other gear such as first aid kits, food, and drinking water are tied into the boat. That way, nothing will float away if the raft flips over.

dry bag

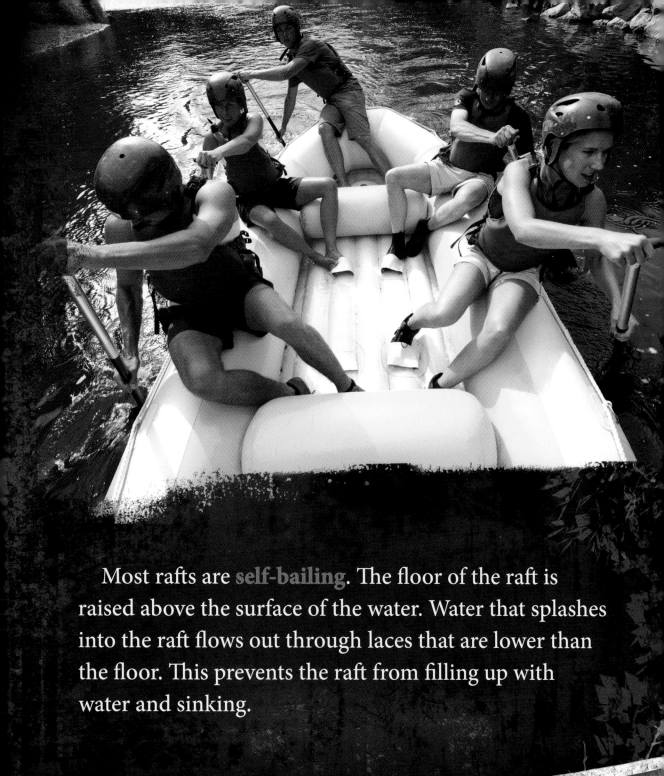

Most rafts are self-bailing. The floor of the raft is raised above the surface of the water. Water that splashes into the raft flows out through laces that are lower than the floor. This prevents the raft from filling up with water and sinking.

Whitewater rafters usually ride in either paddle rafts or oar rafts. Everyone is part of the crew on a paddle raft. Rafters sit on the outside edges of the raft with their feet flat on the floor. Everyone has a paddle. A captain or guide sits at the back and calls out the strokes. These include "forward" and "back." The rafters follow the guide's orders. When the guide calls "drift" or "stop," rafters pull their paddles out of the water to let the raft float.

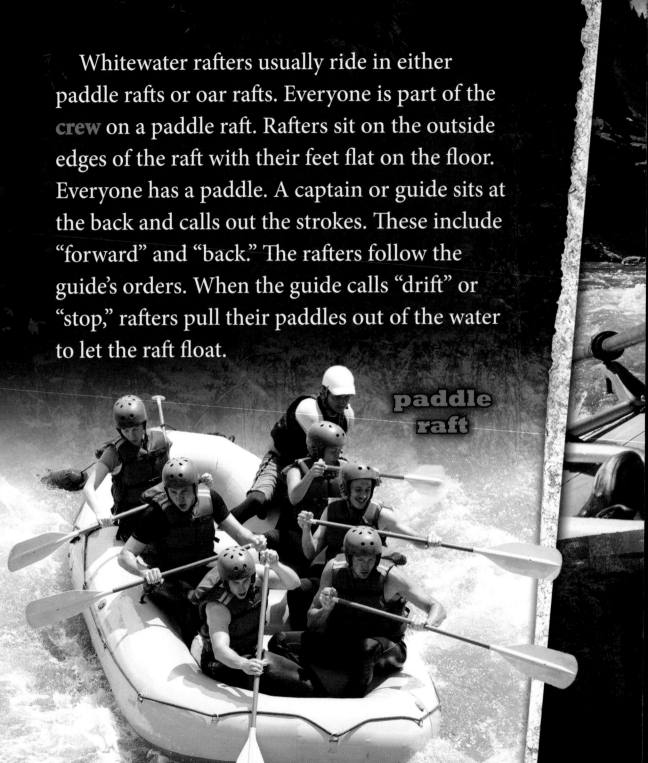

paddle raft

Short on Time?

Some rafters prefer going on motorized rafts. These boats travel faster than paddle or oar rafts, especially on slow-moving stretches of the river. Rafters can see more of the river in a shorter amount of time.

oar raft

Other rafts are steered with long paddles called oars. In these oar rafts, the guide sits in the center of the boat. He or she steers and paddles the boat with the oars. Other rafters do not have to do any work. They just hold on and enjoy the ride! On some oar rafts, people have the option to paddle. However, the guide is still responsible for steering.

RIVER OBSTACLES

Rafters use a scale to help them choose the best river for them. People looking for a low-key float choose Class I or II rivers. These slow-moving rivers have small waves and few obstacles. Class III rivers have more obstacles and waves up to 3 feet (0.9 meters) high. Rafters on these rivers should have some whitewater experience. Expert rafters choose Class IV and Class V rivers. They have challenging obstacles, strong waves, and big drops. Class VI rivers are extremely dangerous. Even experts are warned to avoid them.

Sometimes sections of the same river are different classes. This depends on the type of obstacles that are part of rapids. A hole is an obstacle where water flows down over a rock and creates a hole in the bottom of the river. Water from downstream rushes back up to fill the hole. This creates a swirl of whitewater that can trap rafts or people underwater. A narrow, empty space between rocks is called a sieve. Water can flow through a sieve but rafts cannot. This water is powerful and can overturn rafts.

sweeper

strainer

Strainers are usually large tree branches or bushes that have fallen in the river. These obstacles allow water to flow through them, but they prevent the passage of rafts. A poorly steered raft can become pinned against a strainer. If this happens, the current can force the raft under the water. Trees rooted to land that have branches hanging over the river are sweepers. They can sweep people off the raft and into the river.

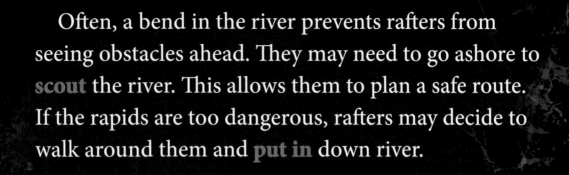

Often, a bend in the river prevents rafters from seeing obstacles ahead. They may need to go ashore to scout the river. This allows them to plan a safe route. If the rapids are too dangerous, rafters may decide to walk around them and put in down river.

A Break in the Action

Rafters who want to take a rest seek eddies in the current. These are places where water flows in a circle, such as behind a rock or other obstacle. Here, rafters can safely park their rafts.

STAYING SAFE IN THE RAPIDS

Before a trip, guides teach rafters basic paddling strokes and cover safety rules. All rafters must watch for obstacles and alert the guide to any dangers. Sometimes rafts flip over or people fall in the water. Guides refer to people out of the raft as **swimmers**. Anyone can become a swimmer. This is why rafters must always wear a life jacket. It keeps a swimmer's head above water. Other rafters can grab the life jacket's shoulder straps to pull a swimmer back into the raft.

Guides train rafters on what to do in case they take an unexpected swim. Swimmers should lie on their backs with their feet in front of them. This is called defensive swimming. It helps swimmers avoid getting their feet caught and softens shocks from bumping into rocks. Then swimmers should wait for a guide to navigate a raft close to them. Other rafters get ready to pull them into the boat. Sometimes, people must swim to shore. For this reason, all rafters should be able to swim.

People should only go rafting in groups of two or more. This way, someone can go for help in case of an accident or injury. Paddles are the most common cause of whitewater rafting injuries. Rafters should keep their paddles down and outside the boat. However, rafters may accidentally swing their paddles during an exciting run. For this reason, rafters should always wear helmets. If a rafter goes overboard, a helmet will also protect against rocks in the water.

What to Bring

Rafting companies usually provide paddles, helmets, life jackets, wet suits, and other gear for rafters. Passengers must bring hats, sunscreen, water bottles, and other personal items.

Rafters enjoy the experience even more when they are in good physical shape. Paddling through fast-moving water requires strength and endurance. To stay comfortable, rafters should dress for the water temperature. Those rafting in cold water dress in layers. They often wear paddling jackets or wet suits. When water temperatures are warm, rafters wear quick drying fabrics. All rafters should wear shoes that can get wet.

WHITEWATER FUN ON THE COLORADO RIVER

The Colorado River has some of the most thrilling whitewater rafting in the United States. The river begins in the Rocky Mountain **wilderness** of Colorado. It winds through Utah and down the western edge of Arizona into Mexico. Depending on where they put in, rafters can float by towering red rocks, mountains, or waterfalls. They may glimpse ancient **ruins** and wildlife along the shore.

The Colorado River offers rafters of all ages and abilities a fun-filled adventure. The most advanced rafters can face Class V rapids in Colorado's Gore Canyon. Here, the river flows furiously down a small waterfall. Rafters must use all of their wits to find safe passage through these roaring waters. For many rafters, paddling Gore Canyon is the ride of a lifetime!

Utah

Colorado

Gore
Canyon

Colorado River

Arizona

N
W E
S

GLOSSARY

canyon—a narrow river valley with steep, tall sides

crew—a group of people who work together on a raft

dry bags—waterproof bags; people put items they do not want to get wet in dry bags.

endurance—the ability to do something for a long time

hole—an obstacle in a river where water flows over a rock, causing a hole in the river bed; water from downstream flows back up into the hole and creates a rush of swirling water.

inflatable—can be filled with air or gas

put in—to place a raft in the river and enter it

riffles—tiny waves

ruins—the physical remains of structures that have been destroyed

run—to raft down a section of a river

scout—to gather information ahead of time

self-bailing—able to remove the water that gets into the raft

sieve—a narrow space between two rocks where water rushes through

strainers—obstacles that allow water to pass through but not boats or people

sweepers—trees that have fallen into a river but are still rooted to the land

swimmers—people who have fallen out of a raft

turbulent—rough and choppy

wet suits—close-fitting body suits that help people stay warm in cold water; wet suits keep people warm but not dry.

wilderness—undeveloped land that is home to undisturbed plants and animals

TO LEARN MORE

At the Library

McFee, Shane. *Whitewater Rafting*. New York, N.Y.: Rosen Pub. Group, 2008.

Pinniger, Deb. *Whitewater Sports*. Pleasantville, N.Y.: Gareth Stevens Pub., 2008.

Young, Jeff C. *Running the Rapids: White-Water Rafting, Canoeing, and Kayaking*. Edina, Minn.: ABDO Pub., 2011.

On the Web

Learning more about whitewater rafting is as easy as 1, 2, 3.

1. Go to www.factsurfer.com.

2. Enter "whitewater rafting" into the search box.

3. Click the "Surf" button and you will see a list of related Web sites.

With factsurfer.com, finding more information is just a click away.

INDEX

The images in this book are reproduced through the courtesy of: Ben Blankenburg, front cover; Douglas Pearson/ Getty Images, pp. 4-5; Maxim Petrichuk, pp. 6-7; KennStilger47, p. 8; Corepics VOF, p. 9; Ammit Jack, p. 10; Fancy Collection/ SuperStock, p. 11; SW Krull Imaging, pp. 12-13; Pichugin Dmitry, p. 14 (left); Momentum, p. 14 (right); Kelly Funk/ All Canada Photos/ SuperStock, p. 15; Giovanni Carlone, p. 16; imagebroker/ Superstock, p. 17; Tappasan Phurisamrit, pp. 18-19; John Warburton Lee/ SuperStock, pp. 20-21.